P9-DNR-318

STAR WARS

THE COMPLETE SAGA

By Jason Fry

SCHOLASTIC INC.

New York • Toronto • London • Auckland • Sydney • Mexico City • New Dehli • Hong Kong

www.starwars.com

SCHOLASTIC
www.scholastic.com

Copyright © 2011 Lucasfilm Ltd. ® & ™
All Rights Reserved. Used Under Authorization.

Published by Scholastic Inc., 557 Broadway, New York, NY 10012

Scholastic and associated logos are trademarks of Scholastic Inc. No part of
this book may be reproduced, stored in a retrieval system, or transmitted in
any form or by any means, electronic, mechanical, photocopying, recording,
or otherwise, without the prior permission of Scholastic Inc.

Produced by becker&mayer!, LLC.
11120 NE 33rd Place, Suite 101
Bellevue, WA 98004
www.beckermayer.com

becker&mayer!
BOOK PRODUCERS

If you have questions or comments about this product, please visit
www.beckermayer.com/customerservice.html and click on the Customer
Service Request Form.

Written by Jason Fry
Edited by Delia Greve
Designed by Rosanna Brockley
Photo research by Katie del Rosario
Production management by Jennifer Marx

Special thanks to Carol Roeder, Frank Parisi, Troy Alders, and Leland Chee
at LucasBooks

Printed, manufactured, and assembled in Menasha, WI, May 2011

10 9 8 7 6 5 4 3 2 1

ISBN 978-0-545-35631-2

10010

Episode I
THE PHANTOM MENACE

Turmoil has engulfed the Galactic Republic. The greedy Trade Federation has stopped all shipping to the small planet of Naboo. While the Congress of the Republic endlessly debates this alarming chain of events, the Supreme Chancellor has secretly dispatched two Jedi Knights, the guardians of peace and justice in the galaxy, to settle the conflict. . . .

Jedi Knight Qui-Gon Jinn and his Padawan apprentice Obi-Wan Kenobi board the battleship of the Trade Federation leader, Nute Gunray, to end the blockade of Naboo. "The negotiations will be short," predicts Qui-Gon. But the Jedi don't know Gunray is working for the evil Darth Sidious, who has told him to kill the visitors.

As Qui-Gon and Obi-Wan wait to meet with Gunray, an explosion rocks the ship. The Jedi draw their lightsabers to face a squad of battle droids. "You were right about one thing, Master," says Obi-Wan. "The negotiations were short."

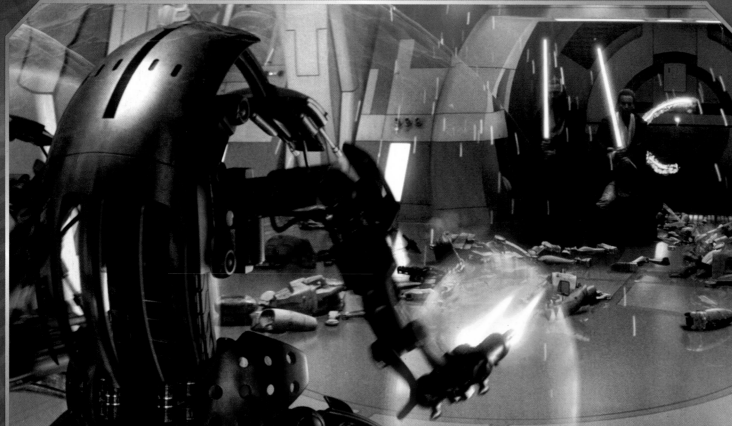

The Jedi slash through the droids and set out to find Gunray on the bridge. When they get there, the doors are blocked. Qui-Gon tries to cut them with his lightsaber, but the Jedi are swarmed by destroyer droids and must flee.

As they escape, the Jedi discover tanks and battle droids being loaded onto ships. The Trade Federation is invading Naboo! The Jedi stow away on the ships. They must get to Theed, Naboo's capital city, and warn its people.

Once on Naboo, the Jedi flee into the forest. They meet Jar Jar Binks, a Gungan who has a knack for trouble. Jar Jar tells them, "The mostest safest place would be Gungan city. 'Tis a hidden city." He offers to take them there.

The Jedi ask the Gungan leader, Boss Nass, for help. He refuses to fight the droid army, but agrees to give them a submarine. "Da speediest way to the Naboo, 'tis going through the planet core," Boss Nass explains. Qui-Gon asks Jar Jar to be their navigator.

Jar Jar and the Jedi set off through Naboo's seas. A giant armored fish attacks their submarine. They narrowly escape when a much bigger monster grabs hold of the fish. "There's always a bigger fish," says Qui-Gon with a smile.

When the Jedi and Jar Jar reach Theed, they discover battle droids have captured Naboo's ruler, Queen Amidala. Qui-Gon and Obi-Wan free the Queen and urge her to come with them to Coruscant, the Republic's capital. The Queen is unsure but agrees to go when her handmaiden Padmé tells her, "We are brave."

Fighting through blasterfire, the group boards the Queen's starship and escapes. Once in space, they must fight their way through the batttleships blockading the planet.

The battleships open fire, damaging the Queen's starship. Astromech droids roll out to repair the ship. The battleships continue to attack, but the feisty R2-D2 makes the repair. The royal starship soars past the blockade!

The ship is still too damaged to reach Coruscant. They need parts to fix their ship. The Jedi decide to land on Tatooine, a harsh desert world ruled by criminals.

Qui-Gon, Jar Jar, R2-D2, and Padmé search for parts in the city of Mos Espa. They stop at a junk shop run by a Toydarian named Watto. He has the parts they need, but he says, "Republic credits are no good out here." He won't take their money even when Qui-Gon tries to trick him with the Force—a mysterious energy field that connects all living things and gives the Jedi their power.

Watto's assistant is a slave boy named Anakin Skywalker. He thinks Padmé is beautiful. "Are you an angel?" he asks. A sandstorm swirls as the visitors leave the shop. Anakin offers them shelter at his house. He tells the visitors that the slaves' masters love to bet on Podraces. A vicious Dug named Sebulba is the best racer in Mos Espa. But Anakin races, too. He has secretly built a Podracer.

Qui-Gon senses Anakin is strong with the Force. He believes he was meant to meet Anakin—just as Anakin believes he was meant to help his new friends. Qui-Gon and Anakin make a plan to get the parts needed to repair the ship.

Qui-Gon makes a bet with Watto: If Anakin wins the upcoming Podrace, Watto must give Qui-Gon the parts for the ship and free the boy from slavery. If Anakin loses, Qui-Gon must give Watto the Queen's ship and Anakin's Podracer.

Spectators cheer as the Podracers line up. R2-D2 watches beside his new friend C-3PO, a protocol droid built by Anakin. The race begins! The Podracers zoom across the desert plains, but Anakin's Podracer stalls. He quickly restarts his engines and takes off.

The race leads through canyons, where the pilots crash into walls, and Tusken Raiders fire blasters at them. Any mistake could mean disaster! Anakin passes the other racers, until he and Sebulba battle for the lead in the last lap. Sebulba tries to force Anakin to crash, but he holds on. It's Sebulba who loses control. His Podracer breaks apart, and Anakin soars across the finish line!

Watto makes good on his bet—Anakin is set free. Qui-Gon tells Anakin he can come to Coruscant and train to become a Jedi. Anakin is excited, but also sad that Watto won't free his mother. Because she wants a better life for her son, Shmi gently tells Anakin to go.

As Qui-Gon and Anakin return to the repaired starship, a tattooed warrior with a red-bladed lightsaber attacks Qui-Gon. It's Darth Maul—Darth Sidious's apprentice! Anakin runs to board the ship. As it takes off, Qui-Gon leaps aboard, too. Anakin greets Obi-Wan for the first time, and the starship rockets toward Coruscant.

Coruscant is nothing like Tatooine: Skyscrapers cover the entire planet. Its skies buzz with flying speeders.

Queen Amidala and Naboo's Senator Palpatine address the Senate and tell them about the invasion of their planet. But the Trade Federation's Senator demands, "What proof do they have?" Taking Palpatine's advice, Amidala angrily demands a vote: Does the Senate still have confidence in Chancellor Valorum, or should there be a new leader?

At the Jedi Temple, Qui-Gon reports to the Jedi Council. He believes Anakin is the Chosen One—the Jedi who will one day bring balance to the Force. Led by Yoda, a wise old Jedi, the Council tests Anakin. He is indeed strong with the Force, but Yoda says, "I sense much fear in you." Because most Jedi begin training as infants, the Council decides Anakin is too old to be trained. Qui-Gon is angry with the decision, and vows to train Anakin.

Frustrated by the Senate's slow action, Queen Amidala decides to return home to fight the Trade Federation. The Jedi fear the warrior Qui-Gon fought on Tatooine may be a Sith, a group of evil Force-users that they believe had vanished. They order Qui-Gon and Obi-Wan to return to Naboo with the Queen, in case the mysterious warrior attacks again.

On Naboo, the Queen seeks out the Gungans. She asks Boss Nass and the Gungan warriors to help free her people. Boss Nass refuses because Naboo's humans have mistreated the Gungans for years.

The handmaiden Padmé steps forward. "Your honor," she says, "I am Queen Amidala! This is my decoy . . . my loyal bodyguard." Everyone is astonished. She gets down on her knees. "I ask you to help us. . . . No, I beg you to help us," she pleads. Impressed, Boss Nass agrees.

The battle begins! The droid army crosses the grasslands in tanks and transports to where the Gungans—including Jar Jar—are waiting to fight. The droids march on the Gungans, firing blasters while the Gungans load their catapults with energized plasma balls.

Meanwhile, Padmé, the Jedi, and a few others sneak into Theed to capture Nute Gunray. They head for the starfighter hangar, fending off droids as they go. The pilots quickly fly off to attack the remaining battleship above the planet. The hangar doors open, revealing Darth Maul! Qui-Gon and Obi-Wan step forward. "We'll handle this," Qui-Gon says.

The hangar is flooded with battle droids. Anakin takes refuge in the cockpit of a starfighter. With R2-D2 also on board, he charges up the guns and blows the droids to bits. But his starfighter is on autopilot, and it roars out of the hangar toward space. Four battles are soon being fought at the same time!

Qui-Gon and Obi-Wan duel the powerful Darth Maul. Obi-Wan is knocked down. He races to rejoin the fight but is trapped on the wrong side of an energy gate. "Nooooo!" Obi-Wan screams as Maul defeats Qui-Gon.

Obi-Wan waits for the energy gate to open so he can avenge Qui-Gon. When it does, he attacks Darth Maul furiously. But Maul disarms him, knocking him into a deep pit. Obi-Wan grabs hold of the ledge. Summoning the Force, he leaps into the air, calling his Master's lightsaber into his hand. He slices through Darth Maul!

The battle on the grasslands rages. A squad of battle droids surrounds Jar Jar and the Gungans, forcing them to surrender.

Padmé and her guards fight their way to the throne room, blasting droids at every turn. They surround Gunray, taking him captive.

Anakin and R2-D2 join the assault on the battleship above the planet. But Anakin's ship is hit. He spins out of control and lands inside the larger ship's hangar. Anakin manages to fire a proton torpedo at the droids that surround him. The shot rips into the battleship's main reactor. Anakin and R2-D2 escape just as the battleship explodes. Without power from the ship above, the droids surrounding the Gungans shut down. The battle is won!

17

Palpatine, Yoda, and other Jedi Masters soon arrive on Naboo. Yoda rewards Obi-Wan by granting him the title of Jedi Knight. He also honors Qui-Gon's wishes and agrees to let Obi-Wan train Anakin to be a Jedi. "The Chosen One the boy may be," he warns, "but nevertheless, grave danger I fear in his training."

Saddened by Qui-Gon's death, the Jedi gather to pay their respects. But the mystery of Darth Maul and the return of the Sith overshadow the ceremony. There have always been two Sith—a Master and an apprentice. But which did Obi-Wan destroy: the Master or the apprentice?

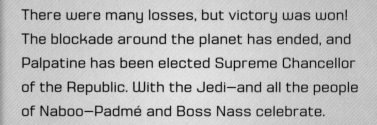

There were many losses, but victory was won! The blockade around the planet has ended, and Palpatine has been elected Supreme Chancellor of the Republic. With the Jedi—and all the people of Naboo—Padmé and Boss Nass celebrate.

Episode II
ATTACK OF THE CLONES

Several thousand solar systems have declared their intentions to leave the Republic. This Separatist movement, under the leadership of Count Dooku, has made it difficult for the limited number of Jedi Knights to maintain peace and order. Naboo's Senator Padmé Amidala is returning to the Senate to vote on the critical issue of creating an Army of the Republic to assist the overwhelmed Jedi. . . .

Ten years after the Battle of Naboo, the Jedi Knights are no closer to solving the mystery of the Sith. They now have another mystery. Several assassination attempts have been made against Senator Padmé Amidala. "In grave danger you are," Yoda warns. Supreme Chancellor Palpatine asks Jedi Knight Obi-Wan Kenobi and Padawan Anakin Skywalker to protect Padmé. The Jedi reunite with Jar Jar Binks, R2-D2, and Padmé. But Anakin is disappointed. "I've thought about her every day since we parted," he says, "and she's forgotten about me completely."

While the Jedi stand guard, the bounty hunter Zam Wesell directs a flying droid loaded with poisonous centipede-like creatures into Padmé's bedroom. Anakin flinches. "I sense it, too!" Obi-Wan says. Anakin leaps to defend Padmé, while Obi-Wan grabs the droid and hangs on as it flies into the night.

Anakin borrows an airspeeder and races to Obi-Wan's rescue. The Jedi chase Zam across Coruscant's packed aerial freeways. She crashes her speeder and flees into a cantina. Anakin and Obi-Wan follow.

Zam tries to shoot Obi-Wan in the back and make her escape, but the Jedi is too fast. He severs her arm with his lightsaber. "Who hired you?" Obi-Wan demands. But a mysterious figure in Mandalorian armor shoots Zam with a poison dart. As Zam dies, the mysterious figure rockets away.

The only clue to the identity of the mysterious assassin is the poison dart. Obi-Wan takes it to his friend Dex. "This baby belongs to those cloners," Dex tells Obi-Wan. "What you got here is a Kamino saber dart."

Obi-Wan finds no such planet listed in the Jedi Archives. He consults Yoda, but it's a youngling who solves the puzzle: Someone has erased the planet Kamino from the Archives. Yoda tells Obi-Wan, "Go to the center of the gravity's pull, and find your planet you will."

Meanwhile, Anakin and Padmé travel back to Naboo disguised as peasants. At her family's lake house, Padmé falls in love with Anakin. Jedi are forbidden to form attachments, but Anakin has loved her for years, and now she loves him back. They can't marry because Anakin would be expelled from the Jedi Order, and the Queen of Naboo would order Padmé to leave the Senate. They try to resist their feelings and carry on with their duties.

When Obi-Wan finds the planet Kamino, he is greeted by a Kaminoan cloner. "Master Jedi, the Prime Minister is expecting you," she says. "I'm expected?" Obi-Wan says in disbelief.

Ten years ago, a Jedi Master paid the Kaminoans to create an army of clones for the Republic—that army is now ready for battle. The man whose DNA the Kaminoans used for the clones is a bounty hunter named Jango Fett.

Obi-Wan asks to meet Jango and his son, Boba—a clone created for Jango as compensation for his DNA. Jango reveals he was hired not by a Jedi but by a man named Tyranus. He refuses to tell Obi-Wan whether he's been on Coruscant recently. But Obi-Wan gets a peek at his suit of Mandalorian armor, and he is sure Jango hired Zam. Obi-Wan reports back to the Jedi Council. "Did the Jedi Council ever authorize the creation of a clone army?" Obi-Wan asks. "No," says Mace Windu. They order Obi-Wan to capture Jango and bring him to Coruscant.

Obi-Wan races to intercept Jango and Boba as they flee for their ship, *Slave I*. The Jedi and the bounty hunter battle—lightsaber versus blasters—but Jango and Boba escape. Obi-Wan flings a tracker onto their ship as they take off.

Following the tracker signal, Obi-Wan pursues *Slave I* to the planet of Geonosis. Jango, suspecting he's been followed, ambushes Obi-Wan. Obi-Wan evades the missiles and follows *Slave I* down to the planet.

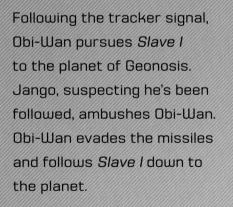

On Naboo, Anakin is troubled by nightmares about his mother. He has not seen Shmi since he left Tatooine. He tells Padmé he must go and help her. "I'll go with you," Padmé offers. Once on Tatooine, they learn Shmi was sold to a moisture farmer named Cliegg Lars, who freed and married her. C-3PO excitedly greets them at the Lars farm! But Cliegg—along with his son, Owen, and Beru, Owen's girlfriend—has bad news: Shmi was captured by Tusken Raiders. "I don't want to give up on her," Cliegg says, "but she's been gone a month."

After landing, Obi-Wan finds the Geonosians are manufacturing another army—of battle droids. He learns of a meeting between the former Jedi Count Dooku and representatives of the Republic's biggest corporations. They agree to lend their armies to the Separatist cause and to help fight the Republic. War is coming!

Anakin sets out to find his mother. He finds Shmi in a Tusken camp, but she is weak and dies in Anakin's arms. Overcome by grief and rage, Anakin ignites his lightsaber and slays all the Tuskens. He returns to the Lars farm and buries his mother. Disturbed by what he's done and his failure to save Shmi, Anakin swears, "Someday I will be . . . I will be the most powerful Jedi ever. I promise you. I will even learn to stop people from dying."

On Geonosis, Obi-Wan contacts the Jedi Council to reveal the Separatist plot, but he is captured by destroyer droids. The Jedi inform Palpatine of the plot and of the fact that the Republic needs Kamino's clones to counter the threat. The Senate grants Palpatine emergency powers, and Yoda prepares to go to Kamino and collect the army.

Anakin is told Obi-Wan has been captured. "The most important thing for you is to stay where you are," Mace Windu instructs Anakin. "Protect the Senator at all costs." Anakin doesn't like the order, but Padmé says, "I'm going to help Obi-Wan. If you plan to protect me, you'll just have to come along."

Together with C-3PO and R2-D2, Padmé and Anakin head for the droid factories. But the people of Geonosis attack them when they arrive. While trying to escape, Anakin and Padmé fall onto a droid assembly belt, are captured, and sentenced to death.

Padmé and Anakin exchange a last kiss as they are led into a massive arena. They are handcuffed to giant stone pillars—along with Obi-Wan. "We decided to come and rescue you," Anakin explains. "Good job," replies Obi-Wan. Count Dooku, Jango and Boba Fett, and Nute Gunray, along with thousands of Geonosians, watch from above as three monstrous creatures are released in the arena.

The executions don't go as planned. Padmé climbs on top of her pillar, picks the lock on her handcuffs, and bashes the vicious nexu with her chains. Anakin leaps to avoid the reek's charge, which shatters the pillar. Freed, he uses the Force and manages to mount the beast.

Obi-Wan gets free, too, and holds the acklay at bay with a spear. He hurls it into the monster's neck.

Padmé leaps down from her pillar onto the back of the reek, behind Anakin. They rescue Obi-Wan and stand triumphant—until a group of destroyer droids rolls into the arena and surrounds them.

All in the arena wait for the execution order. But before Dooku can give it, a purple lightsaber blade appears at Jango's throat. "This party's over," says Mace Windu as a hundred other Jedi appear throughout the arena. But Dooku has reinforcements, too: Battle droids, super battle droids, and destroyer droids march into the arena.

The Jedi clash with the droids, destroying many, but they are outnumbered—one by one Jedi begin to fall. Jango Fett joins the battle and faces off against Mace Windu. The Jedi blocks Fett's laser blasts, and with a slash of his lightsaber, Windu kills the bounty hunter. Both Dooku and Boba are stunned. Boba vows to get revenge.

The Jedi are soon surrounded. Dooku offers them a chance to surrender, but Windu refuses.

The droids raise their guns to finish off the Jedi, but a fleet of gunships swoops into the arena. Master Yoda has brought clone troopers from Kamino.

The battle in the arena spills onto the plains of Geonosis. Dooku and the Separatist leaders flee, taking with them the blueprints for a terrible new weapon known as the Death Star.

On the plains, thousands of clone troopers march on the Separatist droids. Republic gunships rocket through the skies, firing madly at the ships trying to escape.

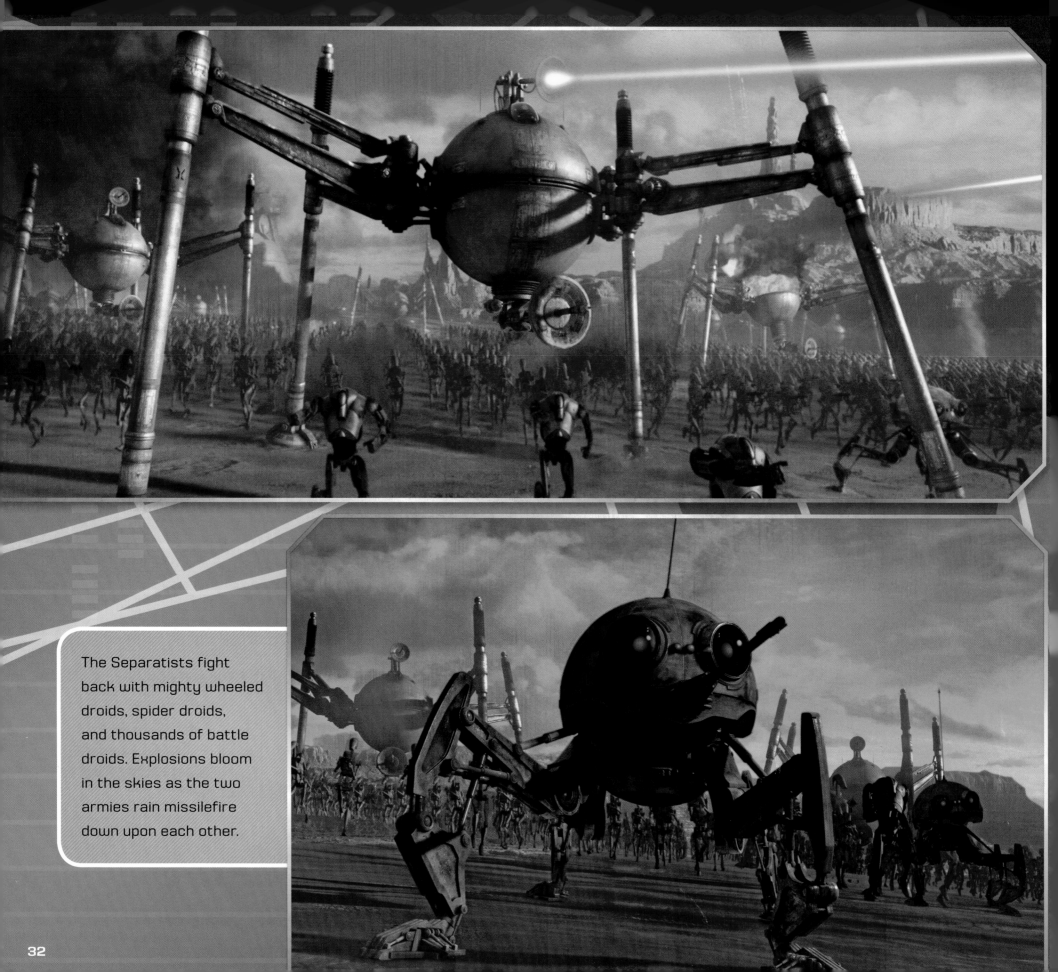

The Separatists fight back with mighty wheeled droids, spider droids, and thousands of battle droids. Explosions bloom in the skies as the two armies rain missilefire down upon each other.

Anakin and Obi-Wan spot Dooku escaping. They follow him to his secret hangar. "We'll take him together," Obi-Wan says. "I'm taking him now!" Anakin replies as he rushes forward to attack. Dooku stuns him with bolts of dark-side lightning, leaving Obi-Wan to fight Dooku. The former Jedi disarms Obi-Wan, and Anakin struggles to rise and battle him again. Dooku quickly bests Anakin, cutting off his lightsaber arm.

As Dooku stares down at his defeated opponents, Yoda enters the hangar. Dooku blasts the Jedi Master with force lightning, but Yoda repels it easily. Dooku then advances on Yoda with his lightsaber, and the two cross blades. Yoda leaps and pinwheels with astonishing speed. Sensing he can't win, Dooku distracts Yoda. He hurtles a huge piece of machinery toward the injured Anakin and Obi-Wan. Yoda stops the piece of machinery with the Force. Dooku uses the diversion to escape.

In a deserted part of Coruscant, Dooku is greeted by his Sith Master: "Welcome home, Lord Tyranus." The hooded figure of Darth Sidious congratulates Dooku on his excellent work. The Clone Wars have begun—just as Sidious planned.

Anakin, meanwhile, escorts Padmé back to Naboo. Despite the obstacles they face, the two secretly marry at the lake house on Naboo as C-3PO and R2-D2 look on.

Episode III
REVENGE OF THE SITH

War! The Republic is crumbling under attacks by the ruthless Sith Lord, Count Dooku. Evil is everywhere. In a stunning move, the fiendish droid leader General Grievous has swept into the Republic capital and kidnapped Supreme Chancellor Palpatine. As the droid army attempts to flee the besieged capital with their hostage, two Jedi Knights lead a desperate mission to rescue the Chancellor. . . .

Anakin Skywalker and Obi-Wan Kenobi weave through Republic battleships and Separatist cruisers as laserfire ricochets around them. Their starfighters skid into the hangar of General Grievous's ship, the cyborg leader of the droid army. R2-D2 quickly identifies the tower where Chancellor Palpatine is being held. The Jedi fight their way past battle droids and destroyer droids to the tower—but Count Dooku is waiting for them.

A rematch! All three draw their lightsabers. "This time we'll do it together," Obi-Wan tells Anakin. Dooku knocks Obi-Wan unconscious, but Anakin, using his newfound strength with the Force, drives Dooku back, cuts off his hands, and claims his enemy's lightsaber. Stunned, Dooku falls to his knees. Palpatine urges Anakin to kill Dooku. Anakin hesitates, saying, "I shouldn't," but he gives in to his anger—and to Palpatine's urging—and Dooku dies.

A moment later, Grievous's ship is hit. Anakin carries Obi-Wan and, along with Palpatine, they head for the hangar bay. But droid soldiers capture them and take them to Grievous. R2-D2 distracts everyone while Anakin and the revived Obi-Wan summon their lightsabers and battle the droid soldiers. When his ship begins to go down, Grievous flees aboard an escape pod.

Calling on his skills as a pilot, Anakin manages to land the burning, shattered ship on Coruscant's surface. "Another happy landing!" Obi-wan says.

Anakin is welcomed as a hero by Coruscant's Senators, though he wants to see only one: Padmé Amidala. In secret, his wife greets him with open arms. "Something wonderful has happened," she tells him. "Ani, I'm pregnant." Anakin is overjoyed, but that night he dreams Padmé will die in childbirth. Frightened by the nightmare, Anakin tells Padmé, "I won't let this one become real."

The Jedi Council and the Chancellor have begun to distrust each other and both sides want to use Anakin. Palpatine tells Anakin he thinks the Jedi want to rule the galaxy. He asks Anakin to be his voice on the Jedi Council, and the Jedi are forced to accept him. "You're on this Council," Mace Windu says, "but we don't grant you the rank of Master." Anakin replies, "This is outrageous!" The Council angers Anakin further by asking him to spy on Palpatine.

Anakin resents the Council's many demands—and he is worried about Padmé. Sensing this, Palpatine tells Anakin the story of Darth Plagueis the Wise, a Sith Lord so powerful he could use the Force to keep those he loved from dying. "Is it possible to learn this power?" Anakin asks. "Not from a Jedi," Palpatine says.

The Separatists' forces have invaded the Outer Rim. Yoda goes to Kashyyyk to help the Wookiees repel those forces. Meanwhile, spies report that General Grievous has retreated to Utapau. The Jedi Council sends Obi-Wan to capture him and end the war.

Obi-Wan lands on Utapau and is told where Grievous is hiding. Obi-Wan confronts him. "Back away!" Grievous orders his droids. "I will deal with this Jedi slime myself!" Obi-Wan faces off against all four of Grievous's lightsabers. But when Obi-Wan's clone troopers arrive, Grievous flees.

The Jedi Council is notified that Obi-Wan has found Grievous. Anakin is sent to inform Chancellor Palpatine of the development. When they meet, Palpatine urges Anakin, "Learn the dark side of the Force, and you will be able to save your wife from certain death." Stunned, Anakin ignites his lightsaber. "You're the Sith Lord!" he says, but Anakin can't bring himself to kill the Chancellor. He decides to hand Palpatine over to the Jedi Council.

Back on Utapau, Obi-Wan pursues Grievous. When the Jedi catches up with him, the two battle hand to hand.

In a furious fight, Obi-Wan pries apart Grievous's armored chest plates, exposing what's left of his original body. Furious, Grievous hurls Obi-Wan across the platform. Using the Force, Obi-Wan draws a discarded blaster to him and fires several shots into Grievous's exposed chest. Grievous bursts into flames. "So uncivilized," Obi-Wan says, tossing the blaster aside.

Anakin returns to the Jedi Temple and informs Mace Windu that Palpatine is the Sith Lord they've been looking for. "A Sith Lord?!" Windu says. "Then our worst fears have been realized." Windu and three other Jedi Masters leave to arrest the Chancellor. Anakin is told to wait at the Temple. When the Jedi Masters reach Palpatine's office, they draw their lightsabers—but Darth Sidious ignites a lightsaber, too, and easily kills three Jedi.

Anakin fears that if Darth Sidious dies, so will his chance to save Padmé. He disobeys Windu and rushes to the Chancellor's office, where he finds Windu holding his lightsaber at Sidious's throat. Sidious begs Anakin for help. Windu tells Anakin not to listen, but as he draws his lightsaber back, Anakin panics. "I need him!" he screams. Anakin attacks Windu. Cackling in triumph, Darth Sidious blasts Windu with Force lightning, knocking him out the window.

"What have I done?" Anakin yells, falling to his knees. Darth Sidious asks him to become his apprentice so together they can become strong in the dark side of the Force. "I will do whatever you ask," Anakin says. "Just help me save Padmé's life." Anakin pledges himself to Darth Sidious and takes the name Darth Vader.

For Anakin and Darth Sidious to maintain power, they must wipe out the Jedi. "First, I want you to go to the Jedi Temple," Sidious orders Anakin. "Do what must be done, Lord Vader. Do not hesitate. Show no mercy." With an army of clone troopers, Anakin marches on the Temple. The new Sith apprentice and his troops massacre the Temple's defenders—even the younglings.

Darth Sidious has prepared for this day. The Republic clone troopers were trained for absolute loyalty to the Republic and to the Supreme Chancellor. Sidious contacts key clone commanders and instructs them to execute Order 66—which proclaims the Jedi have betrayed the Republic and must be executed as traitors.

On planet after planet, the clone troopers turn their guns on the Jedi. On Utapau, they blast Obi-Wan off a cliff. He lands in a sinkhole of water. He survives and manages to sneak off the planet.

On Kashyyyk, Yoda senses the clone troopers' intentions to betray him. He turns his lightsaber on them. With the help of two Wookiees—Tarfful and Chewbacca—the Jedi Master escapes.

Anakin arrives at Padmé's apartment and finds her in a panic. "The Jedi have tried to overthrow the Republic," he tells her. "I will not betray the Republic. My loyalties lie with the Chancellor, and with the Senate, and with you." He leaves for Mustafar, where the Separatist leaders are gathered, to end the war.

Obi-Wan and Yoda make contact with Senator Bail Organa of Alderaan. They decide they must return to the Jedi Temple to warn other Jedi to stay away. Once inside, Obi-Wan and Yoda discover security footage that shows Anakin killing younglings and taking orders from Darth Sidious. "Twisted by the dark side, young Skywalker has become," Yoda says. He instructs Obi-Wan to kill Anakin while he deals with Sidious.

While Anakin destroys the Separatist leaders on Mustafar, Darth Sidious—in his role as Palpatine—addresses the Senate. "In order to ensure the security and continuing stability, the Republic will be reorganized into the First Galactic Empire!" Palpatine proclaims. Padmé and Bail watch in horror as the Senators cheer the announcement. "So this is how liberty dies, with thunderous applause," says Padmé.

Searching for Anakin, Obi-Wan visits Padmé. He warns her that Anakin has fallen to the dark side, and that Chancellor Palpatine has deceived them. "I don't believe you," Padmé says. "I can't." She will not tell Obi-Wan where Anakin has gone. She fears Obi-Wan plans to kill him. Worried, Padmé rushes to Mustafar to find Anakin.

Knowing Padmé may lead him to Anakin, Obi-Wan stows away on her ship. Padmé begs Anakin to run away with her. But Anakin believes they can overthrow Darth Sidious and rule the galaxy together. "Anakin, you're breaking my heart," Padmé cries. "You're going down a path I can't follow." At that moment, Obi-Wan appears. Overcome with rage and believing Padmé has betrayed him, he chokes her with the Force and she collapses. "If you're not with me, then you're my enemy!" Anakin yells. "Only a Sith deals in absolutes," Obi-Wan replies. He ignites his lightsaber and the two face off.

Anakin and Obi-Wan duel through the mining complex, trading lightsaber blows. Their battle leads them across catwalks, up terrifying heights, and down a river of molten lava.

On Coruscant, Yoda confronts Sidious in his office below the Senate Chamber. Sidious blasts Yoda with dark-side lightning, knocking him out. But Yoda recovers and turns the Sith Lord's powers against him. The two battle atop the Chancellor's podium as it slowly rises into the empty Senate Chamber.

Their fight travels across the Senate Chamber, with Sidious hurling Senate pods at Yoda. Although he is a mighty warrior, Yoda realizes he can't prevail. The Jedi Master falls from the podium to the floor of the Chamber. He crawls through the ventilation system to where Bail Organa is waiting. "Into exile I must go," Yoda says. "Failed, I have." And the two flee Coruscant.

On Mustafar, Obi-Wan gains the high ground in his duel against Anakin. Anakin tries to regain the advantage with a Force-aided leap, but Obi-Wan strikes his old friend down. Although Anakin lies helpless on the banks of the lava river, Obi-Wan can't bring himself to kill his former apprentice. He takes Anakin's lightsaber and abandons him. Obi-Wan carries a barely conscious Padmé aboard the ship and leaves the planet.

Left unrecognizable by battle and fire, Anakin manages to drag himself up the lava banks. Sidious finds him there and takes him back to Coruscant. Medical droids construct mechanical parts to replace his missing limbs. They fit him with a suit of black protective armor. This radical surgery completes Anakin's transformation into Darth Vader.

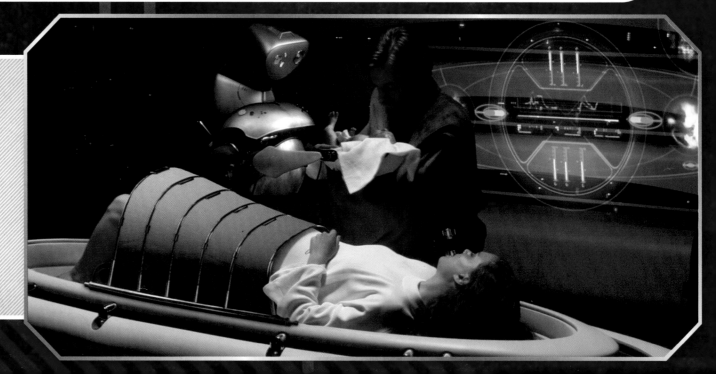

Obi-Wan takes Padmé to Polis Massa, where medical droids try to save her and her baby. But Padmé gives birth to *two* babies, a boy and a girl. She names the twins Luke and Leia. Padmé then grows weak. With her last breath, she whispers, "Obi-Wan . . . There is good in him . . . I know. I know there is . . . still . . ."

Rising from his reconstruction, Vader's first thought is of Padmé. The Emperor tells him, "It seems in your anger, you killed her." Darth Vader screams in horror and disbelief. Sidious smiles a secret, knowing smile.

For now, Sidious has won. "Until the time is right, disappear we shall," Yoda tells Obi-Wan. C-3PO and R2-D2 become the property of the Royal House of Alderaan. C-3PO's memory is erased to prevent him from revealing any secrets. Padmé's body, made to appear as if she is still pregnant, is sent back to Naboo.

For their protection, Leia and Luke are separated. Bail Organa takes Leia to his homeworld of Alderaan, where he and his wife will raise her as their own daughter.

Obi-Wan takes Luke to Tatooine—to the farm of Owen and Beru Lars—and promises to watch over the boy from afar.

Episode IV
A NEW HOPE

It is a period of civil war. Rebel spaceships, striking from a hidden base, have won their first victory against the evil Galactic Empire. During the battle, Rebel spies managed to steal secret plans to the Empire's ultimate weapon, the Death Star.

Pursued by the Empire's sinister agents, Princess Leia races home aboard her starship, custodian of the stolen plans that can restore freedom to the galaxy. . . .

In the nineteen years since the Empire was formed, it has strengthened its hold on the planets of the galaxy. Above Tatooine, a giant Imperial Star Destroyer pursues Princess Leia's Blockade Runner. A laser strikes the ship and disables it.

"We're doomed!" C-3PO frets. "There will be no escape for the princess this time." Princess Leia has survived many dangerous missions for her father, Bail Organa of Alderaan. But this time she's been caught. Aboard the Blockade Runner, members of her crew take up defensive positions.

Imperial stormtroopers blast their way into Leia's ship. Darth Vader leads the hunt for the stolen plans. The soldiers report back that the Death Star plans aren't aboard the ship and no transmissions were made. "Commander, tear this ship apart until you've found those plans," Vader orders, "and bring me the passengers. I want them alive!"

Elsewhere in the ship, C-3PO finds Princess Leia with R2-D2. As the princess slips away, R2-D2 speeds off down the corridor, and C-3PO follows him. R2-D2 boards an escape pod, beeping and whistling that he's on a secret mission. C-3PO doesn't like the sound of that. "I'm going to regret this," he predicts. The droids blast away from the ship, toward Tatooine.

Stormtroopers capture Princess Leia and take her to Vader. "I am a member of the Imperial Senate on a diplomatic mission to Alderaan," she tells Vader. "You are part of the Rebel Alliance and a traitor," Vader insists. "Take her away!" One of Vader's commanders informs him that an escape pod was launched. "She must have hidden the plans in the escape pod." Vader orders troops to go down to Tatooine and retrieve them.

On the desert planet, C-3PO and R2-D2 argue about which direction to travel in and decide to go separate ways.

C-3PO wanders through the dunes before desperately flagging down a sandcrawler operated by Jawas. The same Jawas later capture R2-D2. They sell both droids to Owen Lars, the moisture farmer who lives with his wife, Beru, and his nephew, Luke Skywalker.

While cleaning the droids in the garage, Luke discovers a fragment of a holographic message: A beautiful young woman begs, "Help me, Obi-Wan Kenobi. You're my only hope." Luke wonders if she is referring to Ben Kenobi, a hermit who lives beyond the Dune Sea. When Luke asks to see the message again, R2-D2 says it's a private message for Obi-Wan Kenobi. Before Luke can investigate further, his aunt Beru calls him to dinner.

At dinner, Luke tells his uncle Owen about the message. "I thought he might have meant old Ben," Luke says. Owen tells Luke that Obi-Wan died about the same time as Luke's father. "He knew my father?" Luke asks eagerly. Owen orders him to erase R2's memory. Luke returns to the garage, but R2-D2 has escaped.

The next morning, Luke and C-3PO head to retrieve R2-D2. They catch up with R2 but are attacked by Tusken Raiders, and Luke is knocked unconscious. Ben Kenobi appears, frightening the Tuskens away. When Luke comes to, he explains about R2-D2's mission to find Obi-Wan Kenobi and asks if Ben knows him. The old man smiles and says, "Of course I know him—he's me!"

At his house, Obi-Wan explains, "I was once a Jedi Knight, the same as your father." This is news to Luke, who thought his father was navigator on a spice freighter. Obi-Wan tells Luke he has something for him—his father's lightsaber. "How did my father die?" Luke asks. "A young Jedi named Darth Vader, who was a pupil of mine before he turned to evil," Obi-Wan says. "He betrayed and murdered your father. . . . Vader was seduced by the dark side of the Force."

Obi-Wan plays the message R2-D2 has risked so much to bring him. In it, Princess Leia says she has placed information vital to the Rebellion's survival in R2's memory. She begs Obi-Wan to take the droid to her father on Alderaan. "You must learn the ways of the Force," Obi-Wan tells Luke, "if you are to come with me to Alderaan." Luke says he can't get involved but offers to give Obi-Wan a ride into town.

In the desert, Luke and Obi-Wan discover the ruins of the sandcrawler that belonged to the Jawas who sold him the droids. Obi-Wan concludes that only stormtroopers could have destroyed it. Luke realizes the troopers must have been looking for the droids. He races across the desert and finds his home in flames—his aunt and uncle dead. Returning to Obi-Wan, Luke says, "I want to come with you to Alderaan. There's nothing here for me now. I want to learn the ways of the Force and become a Jedi like my father."

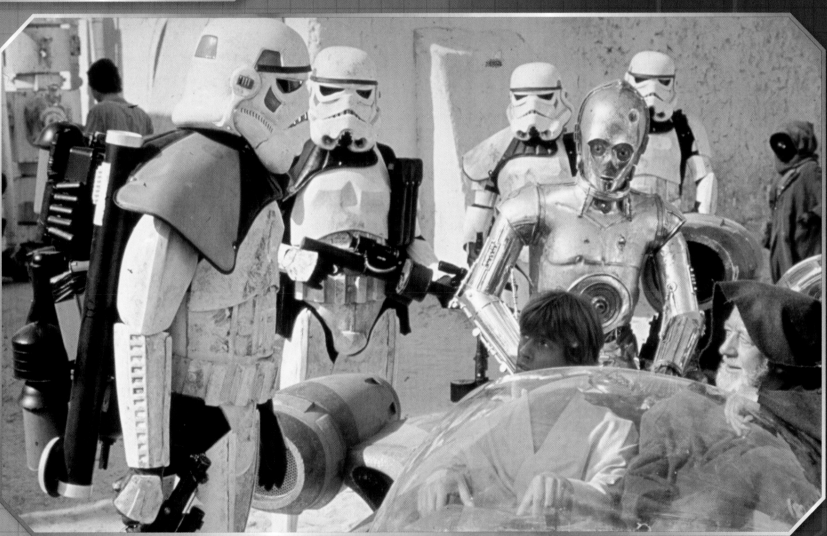

Along with the droids, Obi-Wan and Luke head for Mos Eisley in search of a star pilot who can take them to Alderaan. On their way there, stormtroopers stop and question them. Luke begins to panic, but Obi-Wan uses the Force to trick the soldiers. "These aren't the droids you're looking for," Obi-Wan tells the troopers. "These aren't the droids we're looking for," the trooper repeats.

Obi-Wan leads them to a cantina filled with rough, lawless aliens. There they meet a pair of scruffy smugglers, Han Solo and the Wookiee Chewbacca. Obi-Wan and Luke negotiate a price for passage to Alderaan aboard their ship, the *Millennium Falcon*.

After Obi-Wan and Luke leave the cantina, Greedo, a bounty hunter working for the crime lord Jabba the Hutt, appears to collect the reward for bringing Han in. He holds Han at gunpoint, but the two get into a blaster fight and Han escapes. He heads to the *Millennium Falcon*, andJabba is waiting for him. Jabba is angry that Han owes him money. Han bargains for more time to pay his debt. Jabba agrees but warns, "If you fail me again, I'll put a price on your head so big you won't be able to go near a civilized system."

Luke, Obi-Wan, and the droids board the *Millennium Falcon* just as a squad of stormtroopers arrives. Han blasts the troopers as the *Falcon* takes off. They elude Imperial Star Destroyers and jump to hyperspace on their way to Alderaan.

Aboard the freighter, Obi-Wan begins teaching Luke how to draw on the powers of the Force. "Remember, a Jedi can feel the Force flowing through him," he says.

Still holding Princess Leia captive, Vader interrogates her. But she refuses to reveal the location of the Rebel base. Moff Tarkin, the Death Star's commander, suggests they test the space station's superlaser on her home planet of Alderaan as a way to persuade her. "No! Alderaan is peaceful," Leia pleads. She names Dantooine as the site of the Rebel base, but Tarkin fires the laser anyway, destroying Alderaan.

When the *Millennium Falcon* arrives at Alderaan, the planet isn't there. All that's left is rubble. An Imperial TIE fighter flies by the *Millennium Falcon*, and Han tries to destroy it before it can reach a small moon nearby. "That's no moon," Obi-Wan realizes. "It's a space station." Han tries to turn around, but the *Millennium Falcon* is caught in a powerful tractor beam and drawn aboard the Death Star.

The *Falcon*'s passengers hide in secret compartments. "I use them for smuggling," Han says. "I never thought I'd be smuggling myself in them." Stormtroopers search the ship but find nothing. Han and Luke ambush a pair of troopers and steal their armor.

In the control room, R2-D2 taps into the Death Star computer system. Obi-Wan learns the location of the tractor beam and sets off to disable it. He tells the others to wait for him. But R2-D2 discovers Princess Leia is a prisoner aboard. Luke wants to go rescue her, but Han thinks they should stay put. "Listen," Luke says, "if you were to rescue her, the reward would be . . . well, more wealth than you can imagine." Leaving the droids behind, they head off to save Leia.

The rescue is a mess: Luke frees the princess, but he, Leia, Han, and Chewbacca are trapped by stormtroopers. "This is some rescue," Leia says. She leads them into a garbage masher, but the Imperials activate it with them inside. At the last moment, Luke manages to contact the droids and they shut down the compactor, so the four of them can escape.

Elsewhere, Obi-Wan finds and shuts down the tractor beam holding the *Millennium Falcon* captive. But Darth Vader has sensed his old master's presence and searches for him, hoping to avenge his defeat of long ago. "I've been waiting for you, Obi-Wan," Vader says. "We meet again at last."

Luke, Leia, Han, and Chewbacca head for the *Millennium Falcon* but get separated as troopers chase them. Han and Chewbacca barely escape a squad of stormtroopers, and Luke and Leia swing across a deep shaft to get away. All reunite in the docking bay, where C-3PO and R2-D2 are hiding.

The stormtroopers guarding the *Falcon* suddenly rush away. "Now's our chance," Han says. The fugitives run for the ship, but Luke stops in horror: Vader and Obi-Wan are locked in a lightsaber battle. Seeing that Luke will escape, Obi-Wan stops fighting, allowing Vader to strike him down. Obi-Wan vanishes, leaving behind nothing but his cloak and lightsaber. Luke panics but hears Obi-Wan's voice, "Run, Luke, run." Luke races aboard the *Millennium Falcon.*

With Han and Luke at the guns, the *Millennium Falcon* escapes, blasting four TIE fighters and jumping into hyperspace. "Not a bad bit of rescuing, huh?" Han congratulates himself. "They let us go," Leia says. "They're tracking us." The princess is right: The Empire has put a homing beacon aboard the *Millennium Falcon*, hoping it will lead them to the Rebel base.

The *Millennium Falcon* reaches the base and delivers the stolen plans for the Death Star. The Rebels discover a weakness in the battle station. In order to destroy the Death Star, a starfighter pilot will have to skim the surface and fly down a trench past laser cannons. The pilot must then fire proton torpedoes into an exhaust port just two meters wide. If he can make the shot, it will start a reaction that will destroy the space station. "That's impossible," one pilot says. But Luke disagrees. He takes to the skies as an X-wing fighter pilot, along with R2-D2. Han refuses to help. He takes his reward and heads off to pay Jabba the Hutt.

It's a fight against time and power! In fifteen minutes, the Death Star will be within range to blast the Rebel base. At first the Rebel attack goes well: The Death Star's guns aren't quick enough to hit the small Rebel fighters. The Empire launches TIE fighters to battle the Rebels one-on-one.

"Several fighters have broken off from the main group. Come with me," Darth Vader says, ordering two TIE fighter pilots to join him in a new assault. Chasing down the divided fighters, Vader destroys two groups of Rebel pilots that are trying to hit the exhaust port. Luke and two other X-wings are the Rebels' last hope—and there is only a minute left until the Death Star will strike!

Luke and his wingmen race down the trench. One Rebel fighter is forced to break away after it's damaged. Vader guns down the other, leaving Luke alone as he races toward the exhaust port.

Vader and the TIE fighters close in, but a laser blast from above takes out one TIE fighter. The *Millennium Falcon* has returned! Vader's other wingman collides with him, sending Vader spinning into space. Han whoops in triumph. "You're all clear, kid!" he yells to Luke. "Now let's blow this thing and go home!"

Luke activates his targeting computer. He hears Obi-Wan's voice: "Use the Force, Luke." He turns off the computer and fires two torpedoes into the exhaust port—it's a direct hit!

The Death Star explodes in a massive ball of fire. Han congratulates Luke: "Great shot, kid. That was one in a million!" Luke hears Obi-Wan's voice again: "Remember the Force will be with you . . . always."

Luke, Han, and Chewbacca return to a heroes' welcome. With the droids and Chewbacca looking on, Princess Leia awards Luke and Han medals for their service to the Rebel Alliance.

Episode V
THE EMPIRE STRIKES BACK

It is a dark time for the Rebellion. Although the Death Star has been destroyed, Imperial troops have driven the Rebel forces from their hidden base and pursued them across the galaxy. Evading the dreaded Imperial starfleet, a group of freedom fighters, led by Luke Skywalker, has established a new secret base on the remote ice world of Hoth. Darth Vader, obsessed with finding young Skywalker, has dispatched thousands of remote probes into the far reaches of space. . . .

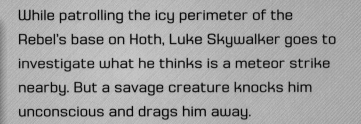

While patrolling the icy perimeter of the Rebel's base on Hoth, Luke Skywalker goes to investigate what he thinks is a meteor strike nearby. But a savage creature knocks him unconscious and drags him away.

Han Solo returns to the base from his own patrol. "General, I gotta leave," Han tells the commander. "There's a price on my head. If I don't pay off Jabba the Hutt, I'm a dead man." C-3PO and R2-D2 interrupt with bad news: Luke never checked in after his patrol, and no one has seen him. Han mounts a tauntaun and heads off to search for his friend.

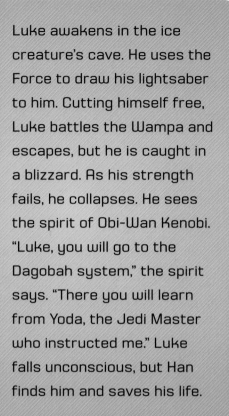

Luke awakens in the ice creature's cave. He uses the Force to draw his lightsaber to him. Cutting himself free, Luke battles the Wampa and escapes, but he is caught in a blizzard. As his strength fails, he collapses. He sees the spirit of Obi-Wan Kenobi. "Luke, you will go to the Dagobah system," the spirit says. "There you will learn from Yoda, the Jedi Master who instructed me." Luke falls unconscious, but Han finds him and saves his life.

While Luke recovers, the Rebels intercept a transmission from an Imperial probe droid. Han and Chewbacca gun down the probe, but the Empire now knows where the Rebels are. "We better start the evacuation," says the Rebel commander.

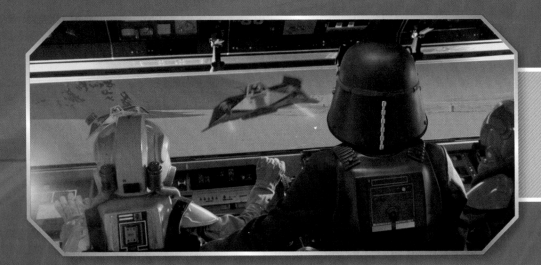

Darth Vader and a legion of warships speed toward Hoth. The Rebels rush to evacuate. Luke and the other pilots leap into their snowspeeders and fly off to defend the base.

Imperial walkers trudge across the snow, attacking the base. The Rebels destroy several of them, but the Imperial assault overwhelms the Rebels. Luke's snowspeeder is shot down, and he is forced to make his way to his fighter on foot.

Han and Chewbacca, meanwhile, struggle to repair the *Millennium Falcon.* As the Imperial soldiers close in on the Rebel base, Leia remains in the command center. She refuses to leave until she knows everyone is safe. "Come on, that's it," Han says, hurrying the princess and C-3PO to the last transport.

A cave-in prevents Leia and C-3PO from reaching the transport. They are forced to flee aboard the *Millennium Falcon* with Han and Chewbacca. They barely get the freighter airborne before Lord Vader and a squad of stormtroopers enter the hangar.

Star Destroyers and TIE fighters pursue the *Millennium Falcon* as it corkscrews wildly, trying to escape. Fighting free of the Imperial ships, Han prepares to jump to lightspeed. "Watch this," he says as he pulls the lever. But nothing happens—the hyperdrive is damaged. "Watch what?!" Leia scoffs.

Unable to escape, Han flees into a nearby asteroid field, dodging huge chunks of rock. The Imperial pilots try to follow but smash into tumbling asteroids. In one of the asteroids, Han spots a deep cavern. He flies the *Millennium Falcon* inside. "I hope you know what you're doing," Leia says. "Yeah, me, too," Han agrees.

Luke escapes Hoth and heads for Dagobah to find Yoda, the Jedi Master that Obi-Wan told him about. When he arrives, he crashes his fighter into a swamp. He and R2-D2 encounter a strange creature that claims to know Yoda. "Take you to him I will," the creature says. Luke follows the creature but is frustrated. "We're wasting our time!" he yells. The creature shakes his head. "I cannot teach him," he says. "The boy has no patience." The creature is Yoda! He's been testing Luke. Luke tries to convince Yoda he's ready. He promises to complete his training.

Hidden in the asteroid, Han and Chewbacca try to fix their ship. But Han is more interested in wooing Princess Leia. She finally admits she has feelings for him. They kiss, but C-3PO interrupts with his usual bad timing.

Darth Sidious, also known as the Emperor, contacts Darth Vader. Sidious tells him there is a great disturbance in the Force centered around a young boy. The Emperor is certain the boy is the son of Anakin Skywalker. Vader is astonished. "If he could be turned, he could be a powerful ally," Vader says. "Can it be done?" Sidious asks. "He will join us or die," Vader promises.

Hidden in the asteroid, Leia discovers space vermin called mynocks chewing on the *Millennium Falcon*'s power cables. Han rushes off the ship and fires his blaster at them. "I have a bad feeling about this," Leia says. The cave shudders. Han realizes they're in great danger. With everyone back aboard, the *Falcon* hastily lifts off. "This is no cave," Han says. They're inside the throat of a huge space slug! They race to get out. The *Millennium Falcon* slips between its teeth—and flies into the Imperial fleet that is hunting them!

On Dagobah, Luke begins his training. Yoda puts him through a series of physical tasks. He instructs Luke, "Beware the dark side . . . anger, fear, aggression . . . A Jedi uses the Force for knowledge and defense, never for attack." To test Luke, Yoda sends him into a cave that is strong with the dark side. In the cave, Luke has a vision of Vader. He draws his lightsaber and attacks the Dark Lord—but Vader's helmet cracks open to reveal Luke's own face.

Aboard his ship, Vader summons a group of bounty hunters, including Boba Fett, to find the *Millennium Falcon*. But one of the Star Destroyers has already found the *Falcon* and is in pursuit.

Han attempts to jump to lightspeed but fails again. With the Star Destroyer closing in, he turns the *Millennium Falcon* around and flies straight at the huge warship. Han attaches the *Millennium Falcon* to the top of the destroyer, where it can't be detected. The Imperials conclude the *Falcon* has jumped to hyperspace. Preparing to follow, the destroyer releases its garbage. Han detaches the *Millennium Falcon* and floats away with the debris. After the fleet is gone, he fires up the engines and heads for the planet Bespin. But Boba Fett is familiar with this trick and follows.

On Dagobah, Luke continues to learn about the Force but finds his lessons frustrating. "You must *unlearn* what you have learned," Yoda insists.

Yoda challenges Luke to lift his ship out of the swamp using the Force. "I'll try," Luke says. "No," Yoda replies. "Do or do not. There is no try." Luke concentrates, but the ship sinks farther into the swamp. Discouraged, he tells Yoda it's impossible. Yoda raises one hand and calmly lifts the fighter out of the swamp, setting it on the shore. "I don't believe it," Luke says. "That is why you fail," Yoda replies.

Han, Leia, Chewbacca, and C-3PO reach Bespin's floating Cloud City. They are greeted by Lando Calrissian, an old friend of Han's. "How you doing, you old pirate?" Lando asks. Bespin's mechanics begin repairing the *Falcon*, but Leia doesn't trust Lando—particularly after C-3PO disappears and then turns up in a junk pile, blown to pieces.

Back in the swamps of Dagobah, Luke has a vision of a city in the clouds where Han and Leia are in terrible pain. "Luke, you must complete the training," Yoda says. Luke decides he must go help his friends. Yoda and Obi-Wan's spirit plead with him, but he can't ignore the vision. "Strong is Vader, mind what you have learned," Yoda tells him. "Save you it can."

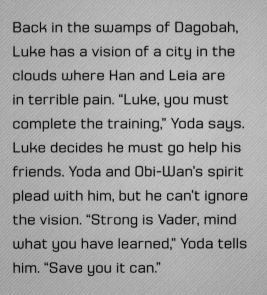

In Cloud City, Lando invites Han, Leia, and Chewbacca to lunch. He's made a deal that prevents the Empire from interfering with his operations. When the door opens, Darth Vader and Boba Fett are waiting. "We would be honored if you would join us," Vader says. "I had no choice," Lando apologizes. "They arrived right before you did."

Waiting in prison, Chewbacca tries to repair C-3PO. When he reactivates him, C-3PO announces that there are stormtroopers here and he must warn the others—but it's too late.

Darth Vader tortures Leia and Han to attract Luke's attention. He tells Boba Fett, "You may take Captain Solo to Jabba the Hutt after I have Skywalker." He informs Lando that Leia and Chewbacca must never leave Cloud City. Lando has no choice. "This deal is getting worse all the time," he mutters.

Vader decides he'll carbon-freeze Luke for his trip to the Emperor—but Lando warns that might kill him. "I do not want the Emperor's prize damaged," Vader says. "We will test it on Captain Solo." His friends watch in horror. "I love you!" Leia says. "I know," Han replies as he is lowered into the chamber. When Han emerges, he is alive but frozen in carbonite.

Vader turns Han over to Boba Fett and orders the chamber to be prepared for Luke. He tells Lando, "Take the princess and the Wookiee to my ship." Lando is angry his deal has changed yet again. On the way to the ship, he disarms the stormtroopers, freeing Leia and Chewbacca.

Leia, Chewbacca, Lando, and the droids race to catch Boba Fett, but it's too late. The bounty hunter takes off with the carbon-frozen Han. They quickly move to escape Cloud City aboard the *Millennium Falcon*.

Luke arrives in Cloud City, where Vader awaits. "The Force is with you, young Skywalker, but you are not a Jedi yet," Vader says. Luke duels Vader, and by controlling his fear he escapes being frozen. But Vader taunts him. "Now release your anger. Only your hatred can destroy me," Vader urges. The Sith Lord is much stronger than Luke imagined.

Vader corners Luke above a great pit. He attacks with his lightsaber, chopping Luke's hand off. Vader urges Luke to join him and complete his training. "I'll never join you!" Luke yells. "Obi-Wan never told you what happened to your father," Vader says. "He told me you killed him," Luke accuses. "No," Vader insists, "I am your father." Filled with horror, Luke lets himself fall into the pit.

Luke slides down a shaft, which ejects him from the underside of Cloud City. He grabs hold of a weather vane and clings to it for his life. "Leia," Luke calls, channeling the Force, "Hear me." Leia hears his call. Dodging TIE fighters, the Millennium Falcon speeds to Luke's rescue.

Unfortunately, the Imperials have disabled the *Millennium Falcon*'s hyperdrive yet again. Chewbacca roars in frustration as Vader's Star Destroyer closes in. But R2-D2 repairs the problem quickly. Before Vader's eyes, the *Millennium Falcon* jumps to lightspeed and disappears.

The *Millennium Falcon* rejoins the Rebel fleet, where Luke is fitted with an artificial hand. He, Leia, and the droids watch as Lando and Chewbacca head off aboard the *Falcon* to track down Boba Fett and rescue Han.

Episode VI

RETURN OF THE JEDI

Luke Skywalker has returned to his home planet of Tatooine in an attempt to rescue his friend Han Solo from the clutches of the vile gangster Jabba the Hutt. Little does Luke know that the Galactic Empire has secretly begun construction on a new armored space station even more powerful than the first dreaded Death Star. . . .

Darth Vader arrives aboard the half-completed Death Star, orbiting the Forest Moon of Endor. He has come to speed up the construction before the Emperor arrives. "The Emperor is coming here?" the commander asks nervously. "That is correct, Commander," Vader says. "And he is most displeased with your apparent lack of progress." "We shall double our efforts," the commander replies.

On Tatooine, C-3PO and R2-D2 travel to the palace of Jabba the Hutt. C-3PO knocks timidly on the gates. Both droids are admitted, and R2-D2 rolls confidently into the fortress as C-3PO rushes to catch up.

The droids meet with Jabba and play him a message from Luke Skywalker. In the message, Luke says he'll soon arrive to bargain for Han Solo's life and presents the two droids to Jabba as a gift. "There will be no bargain," Jabba declares. "I will not give up my favorite decoration." Jabba points to where Han hangs on the wall, still frozen in carbonite.

A bounty hunter then arrives, leading Chewbacca in chains. "I've come for the bounty on this Wookiee," the bounty hunter demands, threatening to blow up the palace if Jabba refuses. Jabba admires the newcomer's boldness and pays the bounty. Guards lead Chewbacca off to a cell.

That night, the bounty hunter slips into the empty throne room and frees Han Solo from the carbonite. Unfreezing is painful. "I can't see," Han says. He grabs at his rescuer's mask. The bounty hunter removes the mask—it's Princess Leia! But before she and Han can escape, Jabba reveals himself. He's been watching. Han is dragged off to prison. Leia is put in chains and forced to become a slave girl.

Luke arrives to bargain for Han's life. "There will be no bargain, young Jedi," Jabba says. He throws Luke into a pit with a vicious rancor. Luke manages to kill the monster and survives. Jabba is angry. He sentences Han, Chewbacca, and Luke to death. They will be cast into the Pit of Carkoon, where they will spend a thousand years being slowly digested in the belly of the mighty sarlacc.

Above the Pit of Carkoon, Luke declares, "Jabba, this is your last chance. Free us or die!" Jabba laughs, but Luke uses the Force to hurl himself into the air. R2-D2, who has kept Luke's lightsaber hidden, throws it to him. A fight breaks out on the barge. Luke and the disguised Lando Calrissian free Han and Chewbacca. Han still can't see, but he accidentally hits Boba Fett and knocks him into the sarlacc's open mouth.

Leia, meanwhile, sees her chance to escape. She pulls her chain tight across Jabba's throat and strangles the mighty Hutt. R2-D2 cuts the chain and frees her.

Luke leaps aboard Jabba's sail barge. "Get the gun!" Luke yells to Leia. "Point it at the deck." Luke fires the gun as they swing to safety. Jabba's barge explodes in a ball of fire behind them.

While the others race off in the *Millennium Falcon*, Luke returns to Dagobah so he can keep his promise to Yoda—and complete his Jedi training. "No more training do you require," Yoda tells him. "Then I am a Jedi," Luke says. "Not yet," Yoda says. "One thing remains. Vader. You *must* confront Vader. Then and only then, a Jedi will you be." Yoda is ill. In his dying breath, he confirms that Vader is Luke's father. When Yoda dies, his body disappears into the Force.

Troubled by the news, Luke tells Obi-Wan's spirit, "I can't kill my own father." "Then the Emperor has already won," Obi-Wan's spirit replies. He reveals another secret: Leia is Luke's twin sister.

Luke returns to the Rebel fleet and finds the Alliance preparing to attack the Death Star—and to kill the Emperor. Admiral Ackbar explains that the energy shield protecting the Death Star is generated from the surface of Endor. A team led by Han will go to Endor and disable the shield, so the Rebel fighters can fly into the battle station and destroy it.

Han's team—which includes Chewbacca, Leia, Luke, and the droids—lands on Endor. They soon encounter Imperial scouts. Luke and Leia take off after them on speeder bikes. Racing through the forest, Luke and Leia stop the scouts, but Leia is knocked off her speeder and separated from the others.

Leia is found by a furry, fierce Ewok. "I'm not going to hurt you," Leia reassures him. Once she gains the Ewok's trust, he leads her back to his village.

Luke, Han, Chewbacca, and the droids encounter the Ewoks, too, but their meeting isn't friendly. The Ewoks take them captive.

The Ewoks tie everyone up and carry them to their village, where Leia is waiting. The Ewoks think C-3PO is a god and decide to sacrifice Luke, Han, and Chewbacca to honor him. Luke uses the Force to convince the Ewoks that C-3PO has magical powers. Frightened, the Ewoks release them all and agree to show them where the shield generator is located.

Luke tells Leia he must leave the others. "Vader's here, now, on this moon," Luke says. "He's come for me. He can feel when I'm near." He tells Leia the Force is strong in all his family—with his father and with his sister—yes, they are brother and sister. Luke insists he can turn their father back to the good side.

Luke surrenders himself, but Vader refuses to abandon the Emperor. "You don't know the power of the dark side," Vader says. "I must obey my Master." He takes Luke prisoner and presents him to Darth Sidious.

Han, Leia, and Chewbacca locate the shield generator just as Lando launches the assault on the Death Star. But the Rebels have stumbled into a trap: The Death Star is operational, and Imperial troops are waiting for Han's team.

Aboard the Death Star, Luke watches the battle station's superlaser target the Rebel fleet. Sensing Luke's anger, the Emperor tells him, "Take your weapon. Strike me down with all of your hatred, and your journey towards the dark side will be complete." Luke cannot resist: He summons his lightsaber and attacks. But Vader catches the blow with his own lightsaber.

On Endor, Han and the Rebels are captured, but the Ewoks strike back. With spears and arrows, the Ewoks defeat the heavily armored stormtroopers. Han blows up the shield generator, clearing the way for the *Millennium Falcon* and the Rebel fighters to attack the Death Star.

ISODE VI: RETURN OF THE JEDI

Luke battles his father. He has grown stronger with the Force since their last duel. The Emperor cheers, "Use your aggressive feelings, boy!" Stepping back, Luke controls his anger. "I will not fight you, Father," Luke says. "I feel the good in you, the conflict." But Darth Vader reaches out with his mind and discovers the secret of Luke's sister. "If you will not turn to the dark side," Vader says, "then perhaps she will."

In a fury, Luke attacks, striking his father and chopping off his hand. Sidious cackles gleefully. "Your hate has made you powerful," he gloats. "Now fulfill your destiny, and take your father's place at my side." Luke looks from Vader's empty wrist to his own artificial hand and lowers his lightsaber. "You failed, Your Highness," Luke says. "I am a Jedi, like my father before me."

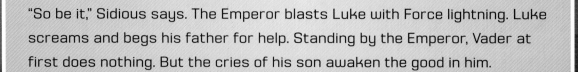

"So be it," Sidious says. The Emperor blasts Luke with Force lightning. Luke screams and begs his father for help. Standing by the Emperor, Vader at first does nothing. But the cries of his son awaken the good in him.

Vader seizes Darth Sidious, sending lightning through his own body, and heaves the Sith Lord into a deep pit. As the Death Star crumbles under the Rebel attack, Luke tries to drag his dying father to a shuttle.

But nothing can stop Vader from dying. "Luke, help me take this mask off," Vader asks. "Just for once, let me look on you with my own eyes." Luke removes the mask, revealing the damaged face of Anakin Skywalker. Anakin smiles at Luke and tells him to flee. Luke insists he can save him. "You already have," Anakin says. He lies back and dies.

With the shield down, The *Millennium Falcon* and Rebel fighters fly into the Death Star's inner core and blow up its main reactor. The ships race back out of the battle station as it begins to collapse. The *Millennium Falcon*, the Rebel fighters, and Luke's shuttle emerge as the Death Star explodes.

Luke takes his father's armor to Endor and burns it to honor him as a Jedi Knight. He then rejoins his friends. The Emperor is dead, and the Rebel Alliance has won. Amid a joyous celebration, Luke sees a vision of three figures: Obi-Wan Kenobi, Yoda, and Anakin Skywalker, now together in the Force.